SEP 2 8 2022

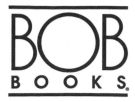

BOB
BOOKS.

Buddy to the Rescue

by LYNN MASLEN KERTELL
illustrated by SUE HENDRA

SCHOLASTIC INC.

*Dedicated to the firefighters of Station 18,
Seattle, Washington*

ISBN 978-1-338-80506-2

10 9 8 7 6 5 4 3 2 1   22 23 24 25 26

Printed in the U.S.A.   40
This edition first printing 2022

"Do you hear that?" says Anna.

Jack and Anna run out the door.

They hear horns. They hear drums.
A fair has come to town.

"Let's get Buddy and go!" says Anna.

Anna and Jack and Mom and Dad
walk to the fair.

Mom gets tickets.
Jack goes on a ride.

"Dad, I want to play a game," says Anna.
Dad plays the game, too.

"Ruff, ruff," says Buddy.

"Buddy, you cannot have a hot dog," says Anna.

Buddy looks big.
Buddy looks small.
Buddy looks like a funny dog.

"Let's go on the bumper cars," says Anna.

Boom! Bang!
Anna and Jack crack and crash
their cars.

"Ruff, ruff," says Buddy.

"Buddy, no! You cannot have a hot dog," says Anna.

Buddy barks.

Buddy runs to the hot dog stand.

Anna sees smoke.
Anna sees fire.

"Dad! Dad!" shouts Anna.

Sound the alarm. Ring the bell.

Call 911.
There is a fire at the
hot dog stand!

The fire truck is on its way.
The siren is very loud.
Red lights flash.

25

The fire truck pulls up.

Water sprays. Smoke puffs.

Buddy is safe. The fire is out.
The hot dog man is safe, too.

Buddy is a hero.
Buddy saw the fire first.

Anna gives Buddy a hug.

The firemen pat Buddy.

"Buddy, now you can have your hot dog," says Anna.